The Peculiar
Miss Pickett

By NANCY R. JULIAN

Illustrated by Donald E. Cooke

SCHOLASTIC BOOK SERVICES
New York Toronto London Auckland Sydney Tokyo

23 22 21 20 19 18 17 16 15   8 9/7 0/8

Printed in the U.S.A.

CONTENTS

Miss Pickett Arrives ... 1

The Magic Shoe Box ... 14

The Glasses Are Lost! ... 24

Miss Pickett Catches a Thief ... 35

The Big Bear Is Lost ... 45

Blue Sawdust ... 61

Fire! Fire! ... 74

Miss Pickett Disappears ... 84

Miss Pickett Arrives

CAROL and Bobby stood and watched at the front window for Daddy to drive up with the baby sitter. Mother was all ready. She was standing by the hall mirror now, taking her gloves off and on, and combing her hair once more.

Carol turned. "You look very nice, Mother," she said.

Since Carol was watching Mother, Bobby was the first to see Miss Pickett.

When Daddy had stopped the car, he came around to open the door for the tiniest little old

1

lady Bobby had ever seen. Her snow-white hair was piled high in a knot on the top of her head. Her tiny face was almost hidden behind a pair of big black-rimmed glasses.

Bobby saw her put two dainty feet—in the strongest, pointed, high-button shoes—on the curb and reach for Daddy's hand to lift herself out of the car.

Miss Pickett stood by the front gate while Daddy returned to take her enormous brown suitcase out of the car. Bobby could tell it was heavy, because Daddy was having to pull and tug to get the big suitcase out of the back seat.

"They're here," Bobby announced, not taking his eyes from the strange scene.

Carol turned back to the window in time to see Daddy still struggling with the heavy suitcase, while Miss Pickett waited impatiently at the gate, tapping a pointed toe.

Then, while both the children watched, Miss Pickett quickly took off her big glasses and gave the gate one hard, straight look. The gate flew open!

Miss Pickett daintily put her glasses back on her nose and started toward the front door with tiny, careful steps.

2

Two pairs of eyes at the front window opened wide, and two small mouths popped open in surprise. What kind of lady was this who could open their front gate just by looking at it?

By the time Miss Pickett had reached the front door, Daddy was close behind her dragging the heavy suitcase. Mother opened the door.

"Come right in, Miss Pickett," Mother said. "I'm so glad you were free to come. Charles and I so seldom go out in the evening, but we do like to have someone with the children when we go."

"Carol, Bobby," she called, "come and meet Miss Pickett. She's going to spend the night because Mother and Daddy won't be back till late. You brought your things, I see," Mother said, watching Daddy struggle through the doorway with the enormous brown suitcase.

With one final effort, Daddy set the big bag just inside the front door. He took out a handkerchief and wiped his forehead while Mother talked on.

"The children had an early supper. Carol's already had her bath, and as soon as Bobby's through with his, they may have the milk and cookies that are set out in the kitchen. They know bedtime is 7:30. The cot in the children's room is made up for you. Just make yourself at home."

Then Miss Pickett spoke for the first time. "We'll get along just fine," she said in the strangest, sweetest voice. "You two run on now and have a good time."

"Good night," Mother said, giving the children a quick kiss while Daddy held the door. "We'll lock the door as we leave. Charles will drive you home in the morning, Miss Pickett. Any special time?"

"I'd like to leave by six," the strange, sweet voice said timidly.

Though Bobby and Carol could see that Daddy

thought that was a horribly early hour, Mother smiled and said, "Fine, good night again."

The door closed, and the children were left alone with Miss Pickett.

"Now, young lady, will you show me where I'm to sleep?"

Carol nodded her head and started up the stairs.

Miss Pickett started toward her heavy brown bag that Daddy had managed to get just inside the door. Very quickly she took off her big glasses, just long enough to give the suitcase a hard, straight look.

Then, putting her glasses back on her nose, Miss Pickett picked up the suitcase as if it were light as a feather and started for the stairs!

Bobby walked behind the tiny old lady, who was daintily carrying the great brown suitcase, as Carol led the way to their bedroom.

When they reached their room, the suitcase fairly jumped on the chair beside the cot where Miss Pickett was to sleep. The children watched while the tiny little lady unpinned a key from the belt of her dress and opened the suitcase.

"I'd like to get out my nightgown," she announced softly as she opened the bag.

Miss Pickett lifted out a bright blue night-

6

gown and a pair of tiny bright blue slippers. Bobby and Carol moved closer to peek at what this curious bag held.

They were almost close enough to see inside the brown suitcase when Miss Pickett suddenly closed the lid. As she did, a strange green cloud of smoke puffed out of the suitcase and went right in the children's eyes!

It didn't hurt, but Bobby's and Carol's eyes were immediately filled with tears. They rubbed their eyes to clear the smoke.

"Curiosity killed the cat," Miss Pickett said sweetly as she locked the suitcase, pinned the key back to the belt of her dress and left the room.

"Now, young man, will you show me where the kitchen is, and your milk and cookies?" Miss Pickett called.

Bobby came quickly, still rubbing his eyes, and Carol followed. Together they went down the stairs and into the kitchen.

While Miss Pickett placed the two glasses of milk and the plate of cookies on a tray, she spoke to Bobby, "Young man, run ahead now and get your bath. I'll bring these up to the bedroom."

"Mother usually fills the tub for me," Bobby said before he thought twice.

"She does?" Miss Pickett looked thoughtful. Then daintily she took off her big black-rimmed glasses and looked once straight at the ceiling. "The bathtub's filled now. Run ahead and be quick as you can."

"But—" Bobby started, "the bathroom's upstairs, and we're in the kitchen and—"

"Never you mind," the sweet voice answered, "the tub's filled, and the water will get cold if you don't hurry."

Bobby turned and trotted up the stairs. Too many strange things had already happened this night for him not to wonder if the tub had really filled itself.

He threw open the bathroom door and there was a tub full of water! His towel was on the chair beside it—all ready for him.

Meanwhile, Carol, in the kitchen with Miss Pickett, summoned all her courage and asked, "How did that smoke come out of your suitcase?"

"My dear," Miss Pickett answered, "I was born during a thunderstorm."

Carol didn't quite see what that had to do with the smoke or the suitcase or the bathtub strangely

8

filling with water, but Miss Pickett said no more. With the tray in her hands, the little old lady started up the stairs.

Miss Pickett put the tray on the bedside table and sat down on a chair between the two beds.

"Into bed with you now, the two of you," she said softly as Bobby came into the room, pink and shining from his bath.

"But, Miss Pickett," Carol complained. "It's only quarter of seven. It's not nearly 7:30."

"It will be," was all Miss Pickett would say.

When the children were in bed, the little lady handed them each a glass of milk. Then Bobby remembered suddenly.

"Mother always opens a window before we go to sleep," he said.

"Which window?" the soft voice asked. "And how far up?"

"She opens that one over there by the desk about halfway," Bobby said, but he noticed Miss Pickett wasn't getting up.

She only turned to face the window by the desk, slowly took off her heavy glasses and looked straight and hard at the window. While both children watched, the window raised itself exactly halfway!

"Drink your milk now," Miss Pickett said, putting her glasses back on her nose as she turned around to face them.

"I don't really like milk," Carol admitted, "but I'd like a cookie."

"No cookies till you've had some milk." Then Miss Pickett noticed Bobby wasn't drinking his milk either.

10

"Two of you who don't like milk," Miss Pickett said sadly as if that were the worst thing in the world. "Well, what do you like to drink?"

"I like chocolate malts best of all," Bobby announced. "Carol always has a strawberry soda."

"A chocolate malted milk and a strawberry soda," Miss Pickett said and took off her big glasses to look once at Bobby's glass of milk and once quickly at Carol's.

"Now, drink your milk," she said again as she put her glasses back on her nose.

Bobby took a sip. "Hey, it's a chocolate malt!" he said in surprise, and took another big gulp.

"Mine's a strawberry soda. Oh, boy!" Carol said, sipping happily.

Soon the glasses were empty and back on the tray.

"Lights out now," Miss Pickett said.

"But it couldn't possibly be 7:30," Carol complained, and then looking quickly at the clock on the dresser, she saw it was exactly half past seven. She snuggled into bed, too surprised to say another word.

Bobby, happily full of chocolate malt, pulled the covers up to his chin and lay back to think over this amazing evening.

"Carol," he whispered, leaning over the edge of his bed, "did yours really taste like a strawberry soda?"

But from over in the dark where they could see a shadowy Miss Pickett getting into her own bed, a voice said, "No more talking now. Good night."

In the morning when the children woke, the cot was neatly made and there was no sign of Miss Pickett or her big brown suitcase.

Downstairs at breakfast, Daddy asked, "Did you two get along all right with the new baby sitter?"

"Oh, yes," Bobby answered, "Miss Pickett did the strangest—" but he stopped in the middle. Did the bathtub really fill with water while they were in the kitchen, and the window really raise itself? It all seemed too magical. Certainly Mother and Daddy would never believe it really happened.

Mother stopped his thinking. "What time did you get to bed?"

"We turned out the light at exactly 7:30." Carol was sure of that, but she was too confused about Miss Pickett and her strange glasses to say any more.

"Well, that's fine," Mother commented. "Next

12

time we go out we'll have to call Miss Pickett again."

"Oh, yes, do," both the children said at once.

The Magic Shoe Box

HELLO again," Mother said, smiling as she opened the door for Daddy and Miss Pickett. "I'll get my coat and be ready. You didn't bring your suitcase, Miss Pickett?"

"No," the tiny little old lady answered. "I brought all I'll need in this little shoe box." She held out a small box that had been tucked under her arm. Bobby and Carol thought Daddy seemed much happier that Miss Pickett had not brought her big brown bag.

"The children are all ready for bed. I told them they might finish the jig-saw puzzle on the dining-room table before they go to sleep. The cot in

14

their room is ready for you, and Charles will drive you home in the morning, just as before. Anything else?" Mother thought a minute, while Daddy held the door. "I guess not. Good night." And the front door closed behind them.

As Miss Pickett turned toward the stairs, Bobby and Carol each took a long, careful look. Just as before, little Miss Pickett had her snow-white hair piled high in a knot on the top of her head. She had on the same pair of big black-rimmed glasses and was smiling the same sweet smile.

Was it possible that this little old lady, just by taking off her big glasses and looking straight and hard, had made the window raise itself, and a glass of milk change into a chocolate malt?

Words came tumbling from Carol's mouth before she could stop them, "Miss Pickett, last time you stayed with us you made green smoke come out of your suitcase, didn't you?"

Miss Pickett looked at Carol in the strangest manner. Her look seemed to say, "Where do children get such odd ideas?" Then she smiled and spoke, "If we have our secrets, then they must stay secrets. Now, I'd like to get out my nightgown."

15

As Carol and Bobby followed Miss Pickett up the stairs, they noticed she was carrying the shoe box very tenderly. For the first time they saw that the small box was tied with heavy string and knotted again and again. Miss Pickett placed the shoe box on the chair beside the cot and began to untie the string. There were too many knots. The tiny old lady grew impatient.

Quickly she took off her big black-rimmed glasses and looked straight and hard at the knotted string. Quick as a wink all the knots untied themselves, and the string flew off the box!

Placing her glasses back on her nose, Miss Pickett opened the little shoe box. She took out her bright blue nightgown and her tiny bright blue slippers. She took out a comb, a brush, and a rather large mirror. She lifted out a soft fluffy pillow, a large box of hair pins and her toothbrush.

How could so much come out of one little shoe box, Carol thought, but remembering Miss Pickett's words, she asked no questions.

Miss Pickett took Mother's pillow off the cot and placed her own big fluffy one in its place.

"I sleep so much better on my own pillow," she said quietly. "Now let's see your puzzle."

The large jig-saw puzzle almost covered the dining-room table. Right after supper Bobby and Carol had started working on it, but it was hardly half finished. Miss Pickett watched, while the children studied the puzzle and placed three more pieces.

"It's supposed to be a picture of the sunrise in the mountains when it's finished," Bobby announced. "Here's a piece of the sun. Where could it go?"

They worked at the puzzle for almost half an

17

hour. Then Miss Pickett suddenly noticed the clock on the wall.

"Gracious, it's twenty minutes after seven. You two must get upstairs to bed," she said.

"But Mother promised we could finish the puzzle," Carol complained.

"The puzzle's not half finished yet," Miss Pickett said firmly. "You couldn't possibly have it done by 7:30."

"But Mother promised—" Bobby said.

Miss Pickett shook her head, but said nothing. She just took off her big glasses and looked at the puzzle straight and hard.

All the pieces on the dining-room table jumped right into place! There was the picture of sunrise in the mountains.

"There," Miss Pickett said as she placed her glasses back on her nose. "The puzzle is finished. Now upstairs and to bed."

Bobby and Carol, too surprised to say another word, started up the stairs. They had just reached the top, with Miss Pickett a few steps behind them, when a loud knock sounded at the front door.

When Miss Pickett opened the door, there stood a strange old man.

From the top of the stairs where Carol and Bobby stood, they could see he had a long white beard that touched the top of his bare feet. He held something heavy over his shoulder. He was dressed in a long white robe and seemed to have come a long way in a hurry because he was quite out of breath.

"Your highness," he said to Miss Pickett and bowed low. Miss Pickett gave a little nod. She seemed to know this strange old man very well.

"What is it?" she asked crossly. "I told them all I was busy tonight and was not to be bothered."

"I know, but the sun, your highness, is terribly confused. Did you want the sun up now? The sun had some idea that it should be over the mountains now. That you wished it that way," the strange old man said breathlessly.

"Oh, dear, no. This is nighttime. The sun's not to come up till morning. That was only a children's puzzle. Wait here a moment, and I'll send the sun a message."

Miss Pickett turned and ran quickly up the stairs and into the bedroom. She ran right past the children, as if they were not there at all.

She opened the shoe box again, and took out the largest book Bobby and Carol had ever seen. She laid it on the bed and turned to a page near the back. Quickly she read the page, then rushed past the children and down the stairs to the door.

"Tell the sun it is to come up at exactly 5:34 in the morning. No sooner, no later. And don't disturb me here again," Miss Pickett said to the old man.

"Yes, your highness. 5:34," he said and suddenly disappeared from the doorway.

"It's exactly seven-thirty," Miss Pickett said be-

fore she even turned around. "Into bed with you two."

The tiny little old lady made sure the covers were well pulled up, said "good night," and turned out the light.

But just before the room became dark, Carol stole a quick glance at Miss Pickett's cot. Sure enough, there was that tremendous book still open on her bed.

When the children woke in the morning, Miss Pickett was gone, and there was not a sign of the big book Carol remembered.

Downstairs at breakfast Daddy looked up from his newspaper, "Sleep well, you two? You did a good job on the puzzle. How was Miss Pickett last night?"

"She was fine," Carol answered. "She—she—she helped us with the puzzle."

Bobby's eyes brightened. "Daddy, look in the paper and see just what time sunrise was today. Please, I want to know."

Daddy found the section that reported weather, tides, sunrise and sunset. He studied for a moment, then said, "The sun rose this morning at exactly 5:34."

"That's just what I thought," Bobby said, giving Carol a wise look.

The Glasses Are Lost!

MOTHER very carefully explained the plans to Carol and Bobby. Daddy had to drive to Greenville on business the next day, and she was going along to do some shopping.

They would leave right after the children were off for school and wouldn't be back till after dark.

Mother had arranged for Miss Pickett to come in the afternoon and stay. It might be after bedtime when they came back, but Miss Pickett had stayed with the children before, and she knew just what to do.

The next afternoon when Carol and Bobby came running into the front yard, there on the porch stood Miss Pickett. Her snow-white hair was piled high in a knot on the top of her head, and her big black-rimmed glasses were firmly in place on her nose.

"Hello, children," she called. "Come in and change your clothes."

"Hello, Miss Pickett," Carol and Bobby answered. "How are you today?"

"Fine," she said as they came into the house, "but I've been terribly busy. There have been a good many storms, you know."

"Yes," Carol said, waiting for Miss Pickett to go on.

Carol had learned that the best way to find out something from Miss Pickett was not to ask questions, but just to look and listen.

While she was looking and listening and changing her skirt, Miss Pickett did go on.

"I just do not like quarrels," the little old lady sighed, "but every now and again Rain does something foolish, and Thunder gets mad, and Light-

25

ning always gets into the fight. And it seems there's no one to make peace in the family but me."

"Oh?" said Carol, waiting for more.

But the tiny little lady shook her head and said, "Dear me, what am I saying? How was school today, Carol?"

"All right," answered Carol. "We learned a new song." Carol stopped and struggled with the zipper of her play skirt.

"Oh, I've caught my zipper. Can you fix it for me, Miss Pickett? It's stuck tight."

"I think so. Step over here in the light."

Instead of taking the zipper in her hands, Miss Pickett simply took off her big glasses for ever so quick a minute, looked hard at the stuck zipper and—whoosh—it zipped right to the top!

"Thank you," said Carol politely in a surprised voice.

When they got downstairs, Bobby already had his chemical set laid out in the kitchen.

"I'm working on a new explosive," he announced. "It says to put a little of this green chemical in with some of this blue, and it should blow up."

26

"Sounds rather dangerous," Miss Pickett said timidly.

"It won't really be a very loud explosion," Bobby explained. "But it doesn't seem to work. I've already put some green in here and nothing happens."

"Put a little more out of the green bottle," Carol suggested.

Bobby carefully added two more drops, and they waited. Still no explosion. Bobby held the little tube high over the sink and added three more drops from the green bottle. They waited, but nothing happened.

"Perhaps I could help," Miss Pickett said quietly and started to take off her glasses.

But even before she had the glasses well off her nose—BANG!—and the mixture exploded by itself.

It happened so suddenly that Bobby dropped the green bottle he held in his other hand. Carol jumped back two feet, and Miss Pickett's glasses flew out of her hand.

"It worked!" Bobby cried happily when the noise was over.

"Boy, what an explosion!" Carol said.

Then the two of them noticed Miss Pickett with her eyes squeezed shut, feeling along the kitchen sink.

"Children, I'm afraid I've lost my glasses. Do you see them anywhere?" Miss Pickett said in an excited voice.

"How can you find them with your eyes shut?" Bobby asked as he and Carol started looking around the kitchen.

"If I were to open my eyes, dear Bobby, the most amazing things would happen." While she spoke, without thinking, Miss Pickett did open her eyes to look at Bobby.

Whoosh—and Bobby suddenly felt himself rise in the air, turn two flips and sit firmly on top of the kitchen door.

"Hey—" he cried in surprise.

But at the same time Miss Pickett's look had gone past Bobby and around the kitchen!

The teakettle on the stove began to whistle "Dixie." The refrigerator door flew open, and the light flashed on and off merrily. The curtains at the windows began to flap and wave as if a tremendous wind were blowing. The washing machine walked right in from the back porch, saying in a thick voice, "At last I get to see what's in this other room."

Quickly Miss Pickett squeezed her eyes shut tight and everything righted itself.

The teakettle stopped singing. The refrigerator door shut tight again. The kitchen curtains were

as before, and the washing machine returned quietly to the back porch. Bobby was standing on the floor again.

"You see, children," Miss Pickett said quietly, "I can't very well open my eyes. You will just have to find my glasses for me."

With that Miss Pickett daintily sat down on the kitchen floor, holding her hands over her eyes now—just to be sure.

Bobby and Carol quickly looked under the sink and behind the door. They looked everywhere for the lost glasses.

"Hello. We're home. We're back!" a voice called from the driveway. It was Mother. They must have gotten back from Greenville sooner than they thought.

"We're in the kitchen, Mother," Bobby called, not stopping his search for a single minute.

When Mother and Daddy opened the back door, they stopped in surprise. There was little old Miss Pickett sitting in the middle of the kitchen floor with her hands over her eyes. Bobby was on his hands and knees searching under the stove. Carol's head was halfway behind the refrigerator.

"What on earth—" Mother started.

31

But before she could finish, Bobby shouted, "Here they are, under the stove."

Very carefully he placed the big black-rimmed glasses in Miss Pickett's hands. Without once opening her eyes, she put the glasses firmly in place on her nose. Then, lifting herself from the floor, she turned to face Mother.

"We had a little explosion," she explained timidly, "and my glasses got lost, but everything is

all right now. I'm ready to go any time you wish to drive me home."

"Fine," Daddy said, still a little surprised at all the confusion.

After Miss Pickett had left, Carol explained very carefully to Mother how they had put a little too much of Bobby's green chemical into the blue, and the explosion had surprised them all.

She didn't tell her mother about the strange things that happened while Miss Pickett's glasses were lost. But always after that Carol was a little more careful how she handled the teakettle, and always managed to close the refrigerator door very gently.

Miss Pickett Catches a Thief

"I ALMOST hate to leave," Mother said as she put on her coat. "Charles, I think we should tell Miss Pickett all about it."

"Do, if you like," he answered, "but after all, we'll be gone only a couple of hours."

Miss Pickett was already settled in the living room. The little old lady had selected a magazine and was sitting in Daddy's armchair by the big lamp.

"Miss Pickett," Mother began, "I think you should know the children were quite excited when I put them to bed. They may wake in the night.

"There has been a thief in our neighborhood lately. He has broken into a number of the houses near here. No one has been hurt. He is just after jewels and valuables, but I thought you should know.

"Charles has made sure all the doors are locked, and since we're only going to the movie, I think you'll be quite safe. We won't be gone more than three hours. You're not afraid, are you?"

"Oh, my no!" Miss Pickett said. "I'll just sit right here and read. You go ahead and enjoy the show."

About an hour after Mother and Daddy had left, in the darkened bedroom upstairs, Bobby whispered, "Carol, are you awake?"

"Uh-uh-m-m-m," was her answer.

"Carol, wake up. Miss Pickett's downstairs, and I'm going down. Do you want to come?"

Carol's sleepy voice said, "Uh? Miss Pickett? Sure, I'll come."

"I'm going to ask her to make the teakettle whistle 'Dixie' again. That was the funniest thing I ever heard. Come on, Carol, if you're coming."

"She'll be angry at us for getting up," Carol said, sitting on the edge of her bed.

"Well, we can always say we wanted a drink of water," Bobby suggested.

"You can get a drink of water up here, and you know it. So does Miss Pickett," Carol answered.

"I don't care, I'll say I want a drink of kitchen water," Bobby said. "Come on, if you want to come."

Very quietly the two children left their bedroom and started down the stairs. The house was quite dark. They could see only one light on in the living room.

At the bottom of the stairs, Carol stopped, "I hear her in the dining room, but it's dark in there. What could she be doing in the dark?"

"Sounds like she's looking for something in the dining room," Bobby whispered, "but Miss Pickett could be doing anything!"

They started to tiptoe through the living room, but at the doorway Carol and Bobby stopped short.

There in Daddy's armchair by the lamp was little Miss Pickett. An open magazine lay in her lap, but she wasn't reading. She was sound asleep.

Her snow-white hair shone in the lamplight, and her big black-rimmed glasses were firmly in place on her nose.

Bobby thought it was strange to see someone

asleep with glasses on, but in Miss Pickett's case he guessed it was the best thing.

Then two pairs of eyes popped open with the same thought. If Miss Pickett was asleep in the armchair, who was in the dining room?

They listened and again heard footsteps. Someone was in there, and it wasn't Miss Pickett!

Very quietly Bobby and Carol tiptoed toward the armchair. Carol touched Miss Pickett's shoulder without saying a word and nodded toward the dining room as soon as the little old lady's bright eyes opened.

Luckily Miss Pickett didn't make a sound. Right away she heard the footsteps too.

Slowly and quietly she got up from the chair and moved toward the dining room. The door was open just enough for three pairs of eyes to peek through.

As soon as her eyes became used to the darkness, Carol saw the man in the dining room. He had put a big sack on the dining-room table and was taking all the silverware out of the drawers.

This was the thief! Carol wanted to run, but felt frozen to the spot where she stood.

Miss Pickett seemed to be waiting for something, and indeed she was. The thief had just put a handful of silver into the big bag and turned toward the drawer for more.

Just as he had both hands in the drawer, Miss Pickett switched on the dining-room light. In the same minute she took off her big black-rimmed glasses and looked straight and hard at the silverware drawer.

With a BANG the drawer closed, and the thief's hands were caught!

"Ouch! What—?" the man yelled. He was dancing up and down with pain and trying to pull his hands out of the drawer. But the drawer stayed shut, and held tight.

"Carol, call the police," Miss Pickett said in a soft voice. Not for one instant did she take her eyes off the silverware drawer.

"Wh-wh-what do I do?" Carol stammered, still too frightened to move.

"Bobby, you do it," Miss Pickett said. "Just pick up the phone and ask for the police. Tell them we have a thief here, and for them to come get him."

Bobby rushed to the telephone in the hall. At first he wasn't sure his voice would work at all, but when the operator answered, he said, "Police. I want the police. Hurry!"

"No hurry," Miss Pickett called from the dining room. "Just be sure they understand you."

"Hello," Bobby said when the captain at the police station answered. "This is Bobby Akin. We've caught a thief. He's stuck in the silverware drawer. Will you please come and get him?"

"YOU'VE WHAT?" the voice on the phone asked.

"We've caught a thief," Bobby repeated. "Come and get him. He was taking all my mother's silverware in a big bag."

"Where do you live, Bobby?" the captain asked.

"I live at 205 East Drive. Miss Pickett says there's no hurry, but come as soon as you can."

"Be right there," the captain answered, and the phone clicked in Bobby's ear.

40

"They're coming right away," Bobby called as he hurried back toward the dining room. "Is he still there?"

"Of course he's still here," Miss Pickett answered. Never for an instant did she take her eyes off the drawer. She held her big black-rimmed glasses in her hand and just kept looking hard and straight at the silverware drawer.

The thief was still struggling to get loose when the police car came screaming to a stop in front of the house.

It was Carol who opened the door for the four policemen.

"This 205 East Drive?" one of the policemen asked.

Carol only nodded, because she couldn't take her eyes off the gun in the policeman's hand.

"Where's the thief?" the captain asked as he came into the house.

"In here," Bobby called. "Come in the dining room."

"Hands up, in there. I'm coming in!" the policeman said as he entered the dining room.

"Don't shoot, copper," the thief begged. "I can't put my hands up. I can't get them out of this blasted drawer!"

Slowly Miss Pickett put her glasses back on her nose and stepped out of the dining room. The silverware drawer opened and the thief's hands were free. But only for a minute, because the captain quickly fastened the handcuffs.

When the other policemen had taken the thief away, the captain questioned Miss Pickett.

"Do you mean he actually got his hands caught in that drawer and couldn't get loose? That's the strangest thing I ever heard of."

"Yes," Miss Pickett agreed. "It is strange, isn't it?"

"But that drawer is just like any other drawer. It opens and closes. How could it have stayed shut so tight?" The captain took off his cap and scratched his head.

"Some things are just hard to understand," was all Miss Pickett said.

The house was full of people now. Some of the neighbors had come in when they heard the police car drive up. Two men from the newspaper were taking pictures with bright, flashing lights. And over by the door, Carol saw Mother and Daddy just home from the movie.

"Mother," Carol cried running toward them. "We caught the thief! Bobby and I heard him, and then Miss Pickett turned on the light and took off her—" Carol stopped in the middle, not sure what to say. In all the confusion no one seemed to notice.

It was almost an hour before the neighbors, the reporters and the police captain left. Mother hurried the children back to bed, and Daddy drove little Miss Pickett home.

The next morning at breakfast, when Daddy opened the paper, there on the front page was a picture of Miss Pickett, Carol and Bobby. A long story of how they caught the thief was right under the picture.

"Well, look at this. Not a bad picture of you two," Daddy said to the children, who were lean-

43

ing over his shoulder. "But you can hardly see Miss Pickett's face behind those big black-rimmed glasses. Wonder why she wears them all the time? They're not at all becoming."

"She doesn't wear them all the time. Sometimes she takes them off," Carol said, winking at Bobby.

The Big Bear Is Lost

WE REALLY must get a new door mat."
Mother said to no one in particular as she waited
on the front porch.

"Uh-mm," Carol answered, not taking her eyes
off her book.

The Stars in the Sky was a book Carol had
brought home from the library. She was learning
many new things about stars.

It was a warm summer evening, and still daylight. Bobby was out playing somewhere, but Carol and Mother sat together on the front porch.

"What did you say?" Carol turned, realizing her mother had spoken.

"Just that we need a new door mat," her mother answered. "This one's all frayed and worn. Oh, here they come!"

The car stopped at the curb, and Daddy got out to open the door for little Miss Pickett. The tiny little old lady stepped daintily out of the car with a shoe box under her arm, for she had come to spend the night. Her big black-rimmed glasses were firmly in place on her nose.

"Good evening, Miss Pickett," Mother greeted her. "Hasn't it been a lovely day? I see you brought your things. The bed's all ready for you. We shall very likely be quite late tonight."

Carol marked her place in her book and stood up to speak to Miss Pickett.

"Now, where's Bobby?" Mother said. "We don't want to leave till he's home. Bob-by! Bob-by!" She called louder and louder. "Bobby, come home now! Bob-by, we're ready to go!"

Bobby didn't appear. He could be down the block in Mike's back yard, or over in the school

playground. But wherever he was, he didn't come.

"If he doesn't hurry, we'll be late," Daddy said. Then he called, "Rob-ert! Robert, we're waiting for you!"

Mother and Daddy stepped off the porch into the front yard and called even louder.

"Bob-by!" called Mother.

"Robert!" called Daddy.

Then Carol saw Miss Pickett slowly take her

47

big black-rimmed glasses from her nose and look just once all around the neighborhood.

Down the street came Bobby in a big hurry. It was as if a great wind were pushing him, and he couldn't stop. Bobby blew right up to the front gate and sat down with a bump. Miss Pickett's glasses were back on her nose now.

"I was right in the middle of a game," Bobby said, picking himself up and looking at the ping-pong paddle still in his hand, "but I came anyway."

Bobby wasn't quite sure how, but Carol had seen Miss Pickett take off her heavy glasses, and she knew.

"Good, Bobby," Mother said. "You can return the paddle tomorrow. We wanted you to be at home before we left. Besides, it's almost seven o'clock. Good night, all." Mother and Daddy were in the car and on their way.

Miss Pickett turned and entered the house.

"It's time," was all she said, but Bobby and Carol understood and followed her up the stairs.

While the children got ready for bed, the little old lady opened her shoe box and took out her bright blue nightgown, her tiny bright blue slippers and her fluffy pillow.

48

She was just placing them on her cot when Carol spoke, "Miss Pickett, this book I got from the library is all about stars. There's a picture of a comet on page 15, and the chapter I'm reading now is all about constellations. But I don't quite understand constellations."

"Long ago," Miss Pickett said, "people didn't know what the stars were or how they got in the sky, so the people made up stories about them. One group of stars they called a hunter and another a scorpion."

"Those things aren't really in the sky, are they?" Carol questioned. "It's just some stories people made up, isn't it?"

"That's what the books tell us," Miss Pickett said. "Does your book mention the Big Bear and the Little Bear?"

"Yes, only it has another name for them too. It's right here somewhere," Carol answered as she looked quickly through the book. "It calls them the Big and Little Dippers."

"There are two names, but they're the same constellations, Come over here by the window and I can show you those two. They're always in the sky," Miss Pickett said.

49

It was just getting dark enough to see the stars. Carol stood close beside Miss Pickett while she pointed toward the north.

"Let me see the bears too," Bobby cried as he joined them at the window.

"That group of stars right there," Miss Pickett said, "make up the Little Bear and right above them, that other group—what—what in heaven—?"

Miss Pickett never finished her sentence, but Carol and Bobby could tell by her voice that something terrible was wrong. Carol noticed too that there was no group of stars above the Little Bear!

"Oh, that naughty bear," Miss Pickett said, more to herself than anyone else. "Quickly, children, get your bathrobes and slippers on. I can't leave you here alone, and I have work to do. You'll have to go with me."

Without another word Miss Pickett turned to her shoe box and took out the longest black cape the children had ever seen. Quickly she slipped it over her shoulders. It covered all of her, from her chin to the tips of her tiny pointed shoes.

Then she took out a tall black hat and placed it firmly on her snow-white hair. Bobby noticed

50

the hat had shiny little stars scattered all over it.

"Into your bathrobes, quickly," Miss Pickett spoke to the startled children. "We have no time to lose."

Bobby and Carol were in their bathrobes in a jiffy. As soon as their slippers were on, they chased after Miss Pickett, who was already halfway down the stairs.

"We can't possibly walk," Miss Pickett said as she opened the front door. "Here. This will do. Stand close beside me now."

Miss Pickett planted herself right in the middle of the door mat. Bobby stood on one side, Carol on the other.

Without another word, she took off her big black-rimmed glasses and looked one hard, straight look at the old door mat.

The door mat began to move! It lifted a few feet off the ground and moved right down the front walk, out the gate and down the street.

Bobby and Carol saw Mike's house and the school playground as they floated past. The old door mat began to move faster and faster.

By now they were moving so fast the houses

and trees were nothing but a blur. The wind blew through Carol's hair. Bobby felt his bathrobe flapping against his knees. It was quite dark now, and the children held on tight to Miss Pickett.

At last they were out of the city. Maybe they passed through several cities, Carol couldn't be sure. Suddenly the door mat began to slow down. It stopped right at the edge of a great forest.

"You must come with me. You won't be safe here alone," Miss Pickett said, stepping off the door mat.

Bobby and Carol were beside her in an instant. Together they started off through the forest.

Miss Pickett led them to a large clearing near the center of the forest. There beside an old log by the light of the moon, Carol and Bobby saw all the bears. More bears than they had ever seen! They all seemed to be very busy around the big log. Then Carol smelled the honey. The bears were having a feast.

"Don't be afraid, children," Miss Pickett said softly. "Stay close beside me."

Then the little old lady took off her big glasses and put them in the pocket of her big black cape. Never had Bobby or Carol seen Miss Pickett put her glasses away! She stepped right up beside the bears and said in a loud firm voice, "I am here."

As if by signal all the bears stepped back from the big log and bowed low.

"In a line, now," Miss Pickett commanded. "I'm looking for the Big Bear, and I've a feeling he's here among you."

With much shuffling of heavy feet, the bears lined up in a single line. The line of bears stretched from one edge of the clearing to the other.

Then very slowly Miss Pickett, with Carol and Bobby as close beside her as they could get, walked down the line. She looked very carefully at each bear she passed.

To Bobby all the bears looked exactly alike. Oh, some were a little smaller than others, and some still had honey on their big paws; but they all had tiny furry ears, and great brown faces, and heavy clawed paws.

Miss Pickett was almost to the end of the line

when she stopped. "Here you are," she said. "What do you mean leaving your place!"

The great brown bear, the biggest in all the line, hung his head as little Miss Pickett scolded him.

Carol noticed one difference between this big bear and all the others. This bear's eyes sparkled like stars!

"You have no business being here. I just happened to look for you tonight, and what did I see? There was the Little Bear in his place, faithful as ever. And then a great space in the sky

where you should be! Right back up there now,
and quickly."

Carol had never heard Miss Pickett speak so
loudly or with such authority.

Then, while Miss Pickett looked straight and
hard at this biggest bear of all with his shining
eyes, the great animal rose slowly from the ground

and disappeared above them in the dark night.

"Back to your feast now," Miss Pickett spoke to the other bears. Then she turned and left the clearing to start back through the forest. Carol and Bobby stayed close at her heels.

Once again the three of them crowded on the door mat. After the old mat had received Miss Pickett's hard straight look, it lifted and started them on their way home. Fast as the wind the door mat traveled!

Before it seemed possible, they were slowing down, passing the schoolyard, and Mike's dark house, then floating up their own front walk. The door mat settled gently right before the door.

Once up in the bedroom Miss Pickett put her big black-rimmed glasses back on her nose, took off her great black cape and tall hat. To Carol's surprise, the great cape and the cap fitted neatly into the tiny shoe box.

"Now into bed, you two," Miss Pickett said softly. "It's later than you think."

Suddenly Carol and Bobby were terribly sleepy. Their eyes would hardly stay open.

"One thing, Carol, before you get in bed," Miss Pickett was motioning toward the window again.

58

"As I was saying, right out there are the Big and Little Bears. That group of stars is the Little Bear and the larger group right above it is the Big Bear. Now, good night."

Miss Pickett was pointing out the window, and Carol through sleepy eyes saw the stars she meant.

In the morning when Bobby and Carol woke, Daddy had already taken Miss Pickett home.

At breakfast Mother was full of news about the movie they had seen the night before.

"It's a splendid picture, Carol. We'll drive you and Bobby down Saturday afternoon so you can see it too. What were the names of those movie stars, Charles?"

"Stars?" Carol repeated foolishly.

"What's the matter with you two?" Daddy asked. "You aren't hearing a word we say. You look sleepy. Didn't you get to bed on time?"

"We were ready for bed even before seven-thirty," Bobby was quick to say.

It was later that evening when the children were once more in bed that Mother spoke to Daddy.

"I got a new door mat for the front door today. That old one was so worn and shabby. But it was

the strangest thing. Bobby wouldn't let me throw
the old one away. He said he wanted it in his
room. Can you imagine any reason why?"

Blue Sawdust

Bobby and Carol were the first in the
neighborhood to see the bright circus posters. The
circus would be in town July 7, 8 and 9! For
weeks they could talk of nothing else.

"When can we go, Mother?"

"Did you get the tickets? Are they good seats?"

"Will Daddy go too?"

"Yes, yes," Mother said a hundred times. "We'll
all four go Saturday afternoon. Daddy has the

tickets. You may keep them in your room, if you like. Your father and I are almost as anxious to see the circus as you are!"

Then on Friday the worst possible thing in the world happened. Bobby had a cold. His face was hot and red. Mother put him right to bed, and Dr. Miller came before supper.

"It looks like a bad one," the doctor told Mother in the hall. "Those pills will break the fever, but young Bobby should stay in bed at least four days."

Bobby heard the last part and cried out loud, "Oh, not four days! I've got to get up tomorrow because we're going to the circus. I can't stay in bed four days!"

After the doctor had left, Mother tried to explain, "You will catch more cold if you go out, Bobby. Besides, you might give your cold to someone else. There's nothing to do but to keep you in bed. I'm sorry you have to miss the circus, but there'll be another next summer."

"Oh, next summer seems a hundred years away," Bobby complained. "Why did I have to get this old cold now anyway." His eyes were full of tears.

"Bobby," Mother went on, "you don't want Carol

and the rest of us to miss the circus too, do you? You'll have to be the best patient you know how. I'll call Miss Pickett to come and stay with you tomorrow afternoon while we're gone. You always like having her here. Do you want to give your ticket to one of your friends?"

"Yeah, I guess so. Give it to Mike. It'll be O.K. if Miss Pickett comes. I won't cry any more. Only I think having a cold is the meanest thing in the whole world."

Carol slept with Mother that night. Saturday morning she called to Bobby from the bedroom doorway.

"What color balloon do you want, red or blue?"

"I don't care," was Bobby's answer.

"Sure you do. I'm going to see everything twice," Carol went on. 'Then I'll come home and tell you all about it. I'm sorry you had to get a cold just now. Mike was real pleased with your ticket. He's going with us. He's sorry you have a cold too."

It doesn't do much good to be sorry, Bobby thought as he lay in his bed. I'm the one who's got the cold. They get to go right ahead and see the circus.

Later Carol called again into the room, "Miss Pickett's here, Bobby. She's coming right up. You'll have fun with her. Let me know if anything special happens, you know. We're leaving now, 'by."

Mother and Daddy both came to say good-by. They promised to remember everything and tell Bobby about the whole circus when they got home.

When the front door closed behind them, little old Miss Pickett, her snow-white hair knotted on top of her head and her big black-rimmed glasses firmly in place, sat daintily on the chair beside Bobby's bed.

"Your mother said you were to drink this juice," Miss Pickett said softly.

"I don't want any old juice," Bobby answered crossly.

"Would you like a glass of water?" Miss Pickett suggested.

"No, I don't want any water either."

"What do you want, Bobby?"

"I want to see the circus!" Bobby cried louder than was really necessary. His eyes filled with tears again.

"Well, if that's all," Miss Pickett said softly. "You shall see the circus."

The way she said it made Bobby wonder, but he spoke through his tears, "Oh, I've got a nasty old cold, and I can't get out of bed for four days. Doctor Miller said so. The circus will be gone by then."

"Never you mind," Miss Pickett continued, "you shall see the circus this very afternoon."

The little old lady walked daintily across the room to the toy chest. The wooden chest was filled with toys that Bobby and Carol had played with years ago, but never wanted to throw away.

Miss Pickett leaned over and lifted several toys out of the chest.

She brought the round blue rug out of the bathroom and placed it in the middle of the bedroom floor. On the round rug she put the toys.

There was an old polka-dot horse. Its tail was ragged and almost pulled loose. When Bobby had been a baby, he had slept with the polka-dot horse every night.

Miss Pickett put the big gray elephant on the rug too, and three small monkeys. She put the horse in the middle of the rug and Carol's old dancing girl beside it.

"Oh, those old toys," Bobby said from his bed. "That's not like a real circus."

"It will be," was all Miss Pickett said. Then before Bobby could protest, she slipped his robe around his shoulders, fluffed his pillows and sat him up in bed.

"The round blue rug is almost like a circus ring, isn't it, Bobby? There are horses and elephants and dancing girls in the circus, aren't there, Bobby?" Miss Pickett said as she sat down beside the bed.

"Oh, but that's not the same," Bobby moaned.

"Now, Bobby," Miss Pickett continued, as if he hadn't said a word, "you take my glasses and look at the toy animals on the rug. I'll look at them without my glasses."

Puzzled Bobby watched while Miss Pickett took the big black-rimmed glasses off and handed them to him. She turned and looked straight at the blue rug.

Putting the glasses on his own nose, Bobby noticed that they just fit. Then he looked at the blue rug, and everything started to change!

The bedroom walls seemed to fall back, and it was just as if he were sitting right in the big main tent. The circus ring was right before him (it still looked a little blue). The band was playing, and the show was about to begin.

"Ladies and gentlemen," a man in a black suit and tall hat called loudly, "you are about to see the most fantastic, the most stupendous, the most gigantic circus ever held! You will see elephants and ponies and dancing girls. You will see the most amazing tricks, the funniest clowns and the most daring trapeze artists ever beheld by the human eye. Ladies and gentlemen, the most fantastic, the most stupendous, the most gigantic circus ever held is about to begin!"

The trumpets sounded and six ponies came prancing into the ring. Each of the ponies had a bright polka-dot blanket over his back. The ringmaster cracked his whip while the ponies

jumped over tables and through great flaming loops.

Bobby saw the whole thing. He saw the elephants, ten of them, holding onto each other's tails and walking in a great circle. He saw them stand on their hind feet and roar, then kneel before the audience.

Bobby saw the clowns set a house on fire right in the circus ring. More clowns rushed in with an old bright red fire engine that puffed clouds

of smoke. He laughed and laughed as the clowns tried to put out the fire with water pistols!

Bobby saw the man on the flying trapeze swing and leap for the net rope. He held his breath till the man was safe on the high platform again.

The dancing girls came riding in on the backs of six ponies. The girls stood on their hands and even on their heads while the ponies trotted around the blue ring.

Bobby saw the whole show. At last all the clowns came back into the ring and bowed so low their chins touched the sawdust. One of them fell over and got his foot caught when he tried to get up.

The circus band played louder than ever, and the show was over.

Bobby took off Miss Pickett's black-rimmed glasses and looked about his room. There on the floor, just as she had set them, were the old toys on the bathroom rug.

He turned to Miss Pickett in surprise, but she was giving him her straight hard look. "You must be very sleepy," she said.

Suddenly Bobby was very sleepy! He lay back on the pillows as Miss Pickett lifted her heavy glasses out of his hand.

"That sure was some circus," was all Bobby had time to say before he was fast asleep.

It was almost an hour later that Miss Pickett heard the rest of the family come in the front door. Carol rushed more quickly than the others straight to Bobby's room.

Carol threw open the door, but Miss Pickett's voice stopped her short.

"Carol, you don't want to catch Bobby's cold," the little old lady said softly. "Stay right there by the door. Besides, he's asleep."

Mother and Daddy were at the door now. They entered quietly.

"Has he been all right?" Mother whispered.

"Fine," Miss Pickett answered, adjusting her big glasses more firmly on her nose. "He's been asleep for the last hour."

"Uh-m-mmm," Bobby grumbled as he woke up. "Uhm? Are you home? How was the circus? Tell me all about it."

"Your cold seems much better, Bobby," Mother said. "You haven't any fever at all."

"I'm O.K.," Bobby answered, "but tell me about the circus."

"Oh, Bobby," Carol cried, "it was the most fantastic, the most stupendous, the most gigantic circus ever held! The big circus ring was filled with blue sawdust and—"

"Blue sawdust?" Bobby sat up in bed, surprised.

"Yes, bright blue, and there were dozens of clowns, the funniest ever. They set a house on fire right in the circus ring and then—"

"Did they try to put it out with water pistols?" Bobby interrupted.

"Yes, how did you know? And, Bobby, the horses all had polka-dot blankets. You remember that old toy horse you used to sleep with? They looked just like that."

"They did, didn't they," Bobby grinned and looked toward Miss Pickett with a wink. But the little old lady was putting on her coat and getting ready to leave. Without a word she went downstairs with Mother and Daddy.

When they had all left the room, Bobby said in a loud whisper, "Carol, I don't mind if I didn't get to go with you. I saw the circus too!"

"How could you, Bobby? You've been in bed, haven't you?" Carol was amazed.

"I did see it in a way," Bobby whispered. "You see, Miss Pickett took her glasses off, and I put them on!"

72

"You put on Miss Pickett's— Oh! That's swell, Bobby. I'm glad you didn't miss the circus. Here's your red balloon," Carol laughed as she tossed the balloon toward the bed. "You didn't get one of those too, did you?"

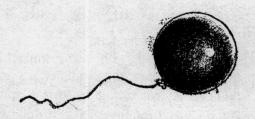

FIRE! FIRE!

MOTHER was going to give a speech at the Women's Club Luncheon. She didn't want to lock the house and leave Bobby and Carol outside, or inside, so Miss Pickett was asked to come and baby sit.

When Miss Pickett arrived, Mother adjusted her hat once more and rushed out the door with a hurried good-by and a hasty remark about "not being late this time."

Though it had been some time since the children had seen Miss Pickett, nothing had changed. Her snow-white hair was piled in a knot on the top of her head, and her big black-rimmed glasses sat firmly in place on her nose.

"School will be starting soon, won't it, Carol?" she asked in her strange, soft voice.

"Just three more weeks," Carol answered. "I'll be glad. Vacation has been long enough."

"Long enough?" Bobby was quick to say. "It couldn't be long enough for me!"

"Well, you two run out and play. I'll just sit here and read," Miss Pickett said, settling herself in Daddy's big chair.

"What'll we do?" Bobby asked Carol once they were outside.

"Get your bicycle, and we can ride through the park," Carol suggested.

"Can't, I lent my bike to Mike this morning. We could roller-skate instead."

Four skates were buckled on four feet in less time than it takes to tell. Bobby and Carol were off down the street toward the park.

But they got no farther than the schoolyard. A crowd of excited neighbors was beginning to gather. Bobby and Carol stopped to see what was going on. Then Bobby noticed the bicycle shed was on fire!

"Hey, Carol, it's a fire. Let's see it. Come on!"
Carol followed Bobby across the street.

"Boy, look at that old shed burn! Has anybody turned in the fire alarm?" Bobby called as they joined the crowd.

"I did," Mike answered, running up beside them, "but they're sure a long time about coming. I was the first to see the fire."

The old bicycle shed was built along one side of the schoolyard, a little distance from the school itself. All last year, when Bobby rode his bicycle to school, he had parked it in this shed.

By now the little building was blazing with a great flame. It wouldn't take long for the old shed to burn to the ground. Luckily there were no houses close to the playground. The only other building in danger was the school.

"Oh," Carol exclaimed, "that fire could spread and catch the school on fire too. Stand back, Bobby."

"Hurry!" Bobby shouted foolishly. "Maybe the old school'll burn too. Then we'd have vacation forever."

"Silly," Carol scolded, "we'd have school just the same. Only all the good books and paper would be burned."

"I don't care. I wish the fire'd get bigger and bigger and burn the whole school." Bobby was too excited to make sense.

"No, Bobby, don't wish the fire would get any bigger," Mike said, as if each word were difficult to get out of his mouth. "Your bicycle is in that shed."

"WHAT? My bicycle is— MY BICYCLE IS IN THERE?" Bobby wasn't enjoying the fire now.

Mike explained, "I was riding it all around the neighborhood and parked it there so I could play baseball with the boys. We had a good game till the fire started. The bicycle's in this end near-

est the school. The fire hasn't reached it yet. I just hope the fire engine hurries!"

"My bicycle! STOP THE FIRE! Stop the fire, quick. My bicycle's in there!" Bobby ran up and down the edge of the playground shouting frantically.

Then Carol had a sudden thought. She knew one person who could put out this fire, even before the fire engine came. In a flash she was off down the street to get Miss Pickett.

"Miss Pickett," Carol called as she skated up the front walk, "come quickly. The bicycle shed's on fire. The school and Bobby's bicycle may burn too. Hurry, Miss Pickett!"

The little old lady popped out the front door and said, "What's that, Carol? What about a fire?"

Carol pulled Miss Pickett along behind her and hurried back toward the schoolyard. Miss Pickett seemed to move awfully fast for such an old lady, but Carol had no time to wonder. On the way she explained everything again.

"The bicycle shed in the schoolyard is on fire. Bobby's bicycle is in there. The fire looks like it might spread to the schoolhouse too. You've just got to do something, Miss Pickett. Mike

called the fire company, but they're not here yet."
Carol was breathless by the time they reached the playground.

The crowd had grown bigger now. The bright flames were shooting even higher. Bobby was shouting louder than ever, and still the fire engine hadn't arrived.

Miss Pickett adjusted her big black-rimmed glasses more firmly on her nose and looked at everything.

A wind had started to blow. The long red flames were reaching out toward the far end of the shed. Some flames licked right against the side of the school.

"Stop it, Miss Pickett. Please, put it out," Carol shouted above the noise.

"I can't, Carol, not in front of all these people," Miss Pickett whispered shyly. "But I'll do what I can."

Quickly the little old lady took off her big black-rimmed glasses and looked straight and hard at the fire. Suddenly the wind stopped. The fire went back to one end of the shed and seemed to spread no farther. The long flames no longer reached out over the whole shed, nor licked against the school.

CLANG, CLANG, CLANG, the fire engine came charging up the street.

"Stand back, everybody," the chief shouted. "Hurry, men, this fire could spread and be a bad one."

It took the firemen several minutes to get the hose off the truck, connect it and turn on the water.

All the while, Miss Pickett kept looking at the fire, and the flames spread no farther.

At last the firemen were shooting great streams of water on the bright flames, and the fire began to go out.

Miss Pickett daintily placed her glasses back on her nose and started off down the street.

"Thank you," Carol whispered, but Miss Pickett didn't even seem to hear.

One end of the shed was nothing but a heap of charred blackened boards. The end nearest the school was badly scorched, but still standing.

As soon as the firemen would let them, Bobby and Mike rushed in to rescue the bicycle.

"Here it is," Mike called. "It's hardly touched. Ouch, those handlebars are hot. Be careful, Bobby."

80

Once the bicycle was out on the playground and had cooled off a little, the boys examined it carefully. The paint was blistered on the front fender, and the front tire had melted and was too soft to use, but otherwise the bicycle wasn't hurt at all.

"My dad and I'll get you a new tire, Bobby, honest, and we'll have the front fender painted too. I'm awfully sorry, but how did I know the shed was going to burn?"

"That's O.K., Mike. It could've happened to anybody. Never mind about painting the fender. I kind of like it bumpy like that. Shows this bike has had a real experience."

Together the boys watched the firemen roll the hose once again on the fire engine and fasten the hydrant tight.

"Can't understand why that fire didn't spread," the chief said to one of the men. "I'm surprised the whole shed didn't burn."

"If the whole shed had caught," the fireman said, "the school would have burned too, sure as my name's O'Reilly. Funny thing. It almost seemed as if the fire was under control when we got here."

Bobby listened to the men talk. Then way down

the street he saw Miss Pickett turning through the gate of their house with Carol. Bobby knew why the fire hadn't spread, but he couldn't tell the firemen. They wouldn't understand at all.

Miss Pickett Disappears

CAROL rushed home from school to tell Mother about the P. T. A. meeting.

"It's tonight, Mother, in the auditorium. And you've just got to go. I want you to meet my new teacher."

"I know, Carol," Mother answered. "I got a notice in the morning mail. I've been trying to get Miss Pickett on the phone all day. I want her to come and stay with you, but she doesn't answer.

"Frankly, I'm worried about her. She's such a sweet little old lady, and living all alone like that."

84

Mother shook her head. "Why, anything could happen."

"Something happen to Miss Pickett! Oh, no!" Carol cried. "Let's go and see her, Mother. Maybe she's sick or something."

"When your father comes home, we'll drive over and find out. She hasn't answered her phone all day."

Carol told Bobby what Mother had said. The two children suffered through the hour and a half before Daddy came home.

"Sit down and eat now," Mother insisted. "After supper, Daddy will take you to find out about Miss Pickett."

"But I don't know where she lives," Daddy said.

"You must know! You always go after her and take her home," Bobby cried.

Daddy shook his head. "She always has me meet her on the corner of First and Magnolia. I let her out there too. I really haven't any idea where she lives."

Carol and Bobby were speechless.

"Well, she must live somewhere near there. You three can go to First and Magnolia and ask," Mother decided.

Bobby and Carol had their coats on before Daddy was even up from the table.

At last they were in the car and on their way.

As they arrived at the corner of First and Magnolia, Daddy said, "There's no place I can park. You two jump out and ask in that apartment house on the corner. I'll drive around the block and pick you up in a minute."

At the apartment-house desk Carol spoke to the man, "Does a Miss Pickett live here? She's our baby sitter, and we're afraid something has happened to her."

"No," the man answered. "We have a Mrs. Packard, but no Miss Pickett."

"She must live here," Bobby insisted. "This is the only apartment house in the neighborhood."

"Sorry, I never heard of your Miss Pickett." And the man turned away.

Out on the sidewalk again, Carol and Bobby looked up and down the street. There was a filling station and two grocery stores, but they were all dark. There was no one else on the street except a newsboy standing on the opposite corner.

"How can we ever find her?" Carol sighed. "It

would take all night to go to each house and ask if they know Miss Pickett."

"Hey," the newsboy called, "did you say Miss Pickett?"

"Yes, do you know her?" Bobby ran toward him.

"Sure I know her. Are you Carol and Bobby?"

"Why, yes! How did you know that?"

"Miss Pickett left this note for you. She had to go away," the newsboy said.

Carol and Bobby raced for the bright spot under the street light and looked at the folded piece of paper the newsboy had handed them.

> *Hope your mother can find another baby sitter. I was called away very suddenly. Put this at the very bottom of the toy chest.*
>
> *Miss Pickett*

That was all it said!

"But—" Bobby stammered, "it doesn't say why or where or if she'll be back or—"

"And why would she want us to put this note at the bottom of the toy chest?" Carol wondered.

They heard Daddy honk the horn and quickly ran toward the car.

"Daddy, she's gone out of town. She left a note for us with the newsboy," Carol explained.

"I thought it would be something like that," said Daddy.

They drove the rest of the way home in silence.

Mother wanted to see the note. "Well, I'm glad it's nothing serious. We'll probably never find another baby sitter as good as Miss Pickett," she said.

"No," Carol agreed sadly. "There'll never be another like Miss Pickett."

"Why on earth do you guess she wanted you to put this note at the bottom of the toy chest?" Mother asked. "But you may as well do it. Get ready for bed first, though; it's already after seven." She handed the note to Carol.

It didn't take Carol and Bobby long to get into their pajamas.

Then they started lifting all the old toys out of the chest. Bobby looked sadly at the old polka-dot horse as he placed it on the floor.

"What's this box down here at the bottom?" he asked Carol.

"I didn't know there was a box in the chest. It's a shoe box, isn't it?" Carol exclaimed as Bobby lifted it out. "It's Miss Pickett's shoe box! Open it quickly, Bobby!"

It really was Miss Pickett's shoe box, and in it were Miss Pickett's big black-rimmed glasses.

"That's why she wanted us to put the note on the very bottom of the toy chest. She wanted us to find the glasses," Carol cried. "Look through them, Bobby, and see what happens."

Bobby put the big glasses on his nose, but nothing happened.

Carol put the glasses on her nose. The children waited, but nothing happened.

"I guess the glasses won't work without Miss Pickett here too," Bobby said disappointed.

With the glasses still on her nose, Carol looked at Miss Pickett's note again.

"Hey, Bobby, there're some words here we didn't see," Carol shouted.

Bobby looked at the paper in her hand. "No, it's just the same," he said.

"But through the glasses it's different! Put them on and see, Bobby!"

"Why, it is!" Bobby cried when he had the big glasses on. "It says:

> *Remember a secret is only fun as long as it stays a secret. Put the glasses in the toy chest for me. I'll need them when I come back. And now, into bed, you two. It's exactly seven-thirty.*
>
> *Miss Pickett"*

Carol turned to look at the clock. It was exactly half past seven!

Quickly they put the glasses and the note in the shoe box. They placed the box on the bottom of the toy chest and piled all the old toys on top.

As Carol jumped into bed, she cried, "Bobby, do you realize Miss Pickett said 'when I come back'! Wherever she has gone, she will come back sometime."

"And when she does, she'll know right where to find her big black-rimmed glasses," Bobby said as he turned out the light.